Little Blue Truck

Alice Schertle

Illustrated by Jill McElmurry

HARCOURT, INC.

Orlando Austin New York San Diego London

For information about permission to reproduce selections from this book, please
write to Permissions, Houghton Mifflin Harcourt Publishing Company 215 Park
Avenue South NY NY 10003.

www.hmhbooks.com

Library of Congress Cataloging-in-Publication Data
Schertle, Alice.
Little blue truck/Alice Schertle; illustrated by Jill McElmurry.
p.   cm.
Summary: A small blue truck finds his way out of a jam, with a little help from his friends.
[1. Trucks—Fiction. 2. Friendship—Fiction.] I. McElmurry, Jill, ill. II. Title.
PZ8.3.S29717Lit 2008
[E]—dc22   2006029445
ISBN 978-0-15-205661-2

SCP 9 8
4500404728
Printed in China

The illustrations in this book were done in gouache on
Arches 140 lb. cold-pressed watercolor paper.
The display type was set in Rootin Tootin. The text type was set in PT Barnum.
Color separations by Colourscan Co. Pte. Ltd., Singapore
Production supervision by Christine Witnik
Designed by April Ward

To Jen and Drew, Spence and Dylan,
Kate and John. Beep! Beep!
—A. S.

For Iris, who does her best to get us
from A to B and back again.
—J. M.

Horn went "**Beep!**"
Engine purred.
Friendliest sounds
you ever heard.

Little Blue Truck
came down the road.
"Beep!" said Blue
to a big green toad.

Toad said, "**Croak!**"
and winked an eye
when Little Blue Truck
went rolling by.

TOAD
CROSSING

Sheep said, "Baaa!"
Cow said, "Moo!"
"Oink!" said a piggy.
"Beep!" said Blue.

"**Cluck!**" said a chicken,
and her chick said, "**Peep!**"
"**Maaa!**" said a goat.
Blue said, "**Beep!**"

"**Neigh!**" said a horse.
"**Quack!**" said a duck.
"**Beep!**" said the friendly
Little Blue Truck.

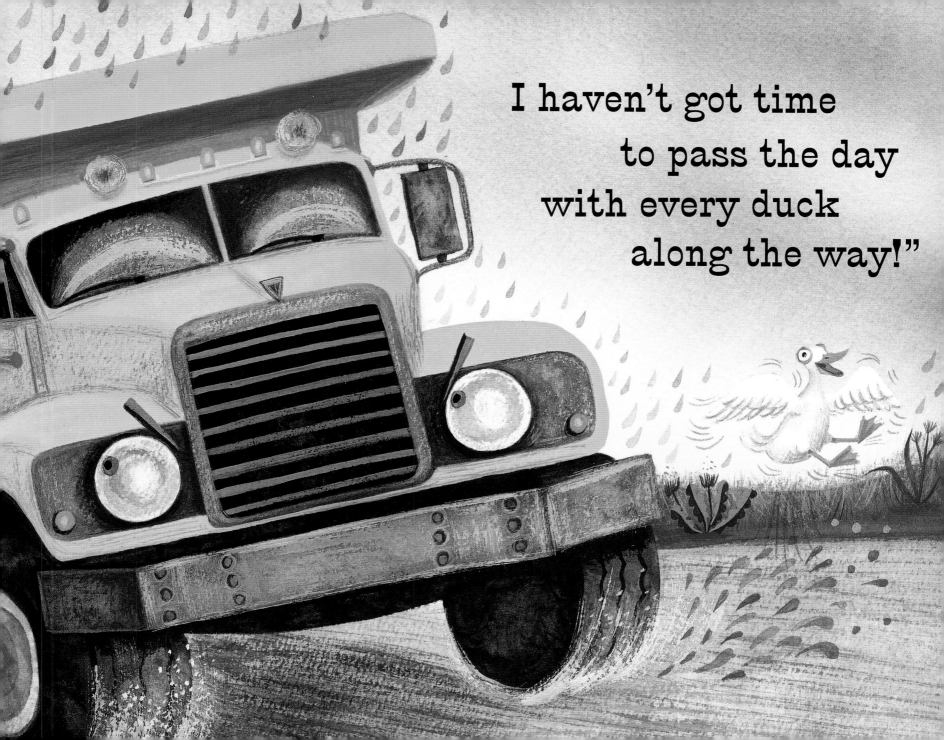

I haven't got time
to pass the day
with every duck
along the way!"

ROOOM! went the Dump
around a curve.
He saw a puddle
and he tried to swerve—

Into the mud
rolled the big fat truck,
and his big important
wheels got STUCK!

His heavy-duty
dump-truck tires
were sunk down deep
in muck and mire.

"Honk!" cried the Dump,
and he sounded scared,
but nobody heard
(or nobody cared).

Then . . .

Into the mud

bump

bump

bump

came the Little Blue Truck
to help the Dump.

Little Blue pushed
with all his might—

now Blue and the Dump
were BOTH stuck tight.

"Help! Help! Help!"
 cried the Little Blue Truck.
"Beep! Beep! Beep!
 I'm stuck! I'm stuck!"

Everybody heard that
"Beep! Beep! Beep!"
 The cow came running
 with the pig and the sheep.

Up at a gallop
ran the big brown horse.
Goat jumped over
the fence, of course.

The hen came flapping
with the chick and the duck,
and everybody pushed
the Little Blue Truck.

Head to head
and rump to rump,
they all pushed Blue—
who pushed the Dump.

They couldn't quite budge
that heavy load.
Then who hopped up
but the big green toad.

All together—
one...two...*three!*
One last push
and the trucks were FREE!

"Thanks, little brother,"
said the Dump to Blue.
"You helped *me*
and they helped *you.*

Now I see
a lot depends
on a helping hand
from a few good friends!"

"Beep!" said Blue.
"Who wants a ride?"
Everybody scrambled
to jump inside.

Oink! Quack! Baaa!
Moo! Cluck! Peep!
Neigh! Croak! Maaa!

Beep! Beep! Beep!